The Tale of Peter Rabbit

and other Favourite Stories

Simplified retellings of the original tales by
BEATRIX POTTER

F. WARNE & CO

FREDERICK WARNE
Published by the Penguin Group
Penguin Books Ltd, 80 Strand, London WC2R 0RL, England
Penguin Young Readers Group, 345 Hudson Street, New York, New York 10014, USA
Penguin (Group) Australia, 250 Camberwell Road, Camberwell, Victoria 3124, Australia
Penguin Group (NZ), cnr Airborne and Rosedale Roads, Albany, Auckland 1310,
New Zealand
A Penguin Company

7 9 10 8 6
Copyright © Frederick Warne & Co., 2007
New reproductions of Beatrix Potter's book illustrations copyright © Frederick Warne & Co.,
2002
Original text and illustrations copyright © Frederick Warne & Co., 1902, 1904, 1905, 1907,
1908. 1910, 1913, 1917, 1922.

Additional illustrations by Elizabeth Catchpole, Colin Twinn and Alex Vining

Frederick Warne & Co. is the owner of all rights, copyrights and trademarks in the
Beatrix Potter character names and illustrations.

ISBN-13: 978-0-72325-928-2
Printed in China

The Tale of Peter Rabbit

and other Favourite Stories

Simplified retellings of the original tales by

BEATRIX POTTER

F. WARNE & Co.

Contents

Peter Rabbit

Naughty Peter Rabbit finds himself in all kinds
of trouble as he squeezes himself under the gate
into Mr. McGregor's garden.

Tom Kitten

Mrs. Tabitha Twitchit dresses her three kittens before
tea in their best clothes. But mischievous Tom and his
two sisters are not going to stay clean for long.

Jemima Puddle-Duck

As Jemima Puddle-duck tries to find a convenient
nesting place, she meets a mysterious whiskered
gentleman who is rather too eager to help.

Benjamin Bunny

When naughty Benjamin Bunny finds that his cousin,
Peter, has lost his clothes in Mr. McGregor's garden,
he decides they must go and retrieve them.

Nursery Rhymes

Beatrix Potter's exquisite sketches and watercolours
perfectly complement this collection of traditional
rhymes and riddles.

The Tale of Peter Rabbit

A simplified retelling of the original tale by

BEATRIX POTTER

F. WARNE & CO.

This is Peter Rabbit.

He lives here with his mother, Mrs. Rabbit, and his sisters, Flopsy, Mopsy and Cotton-tail.

One morning Mrs. Rabbit said, "I am going out, children. Now run along, but don't go into Mr. McGregor's garden."

Then Mrs. Rabbit took her
basket and her umbrella and
walked through the wood.

Flopsy, Mopsy and
Cotton-tail were good
little rabbits. They went
to pick blackberries.

But Peter was a naughty
little rabbit. He ran to
Mr. McGregor's garden
and squeezed under
the gate!

Peter sat in the garden and
ate lots of radishes.

Then, feeling rather sick, he went to look for some parsley to make him feel better.

But round the corner he met . . .

... Mr. McGregor!

Mr. McGregor ran after
Peter Rabbit, waving a
rake and shouting,
"Stop thief!"

Peter ran into a net and got caught by the buttons on his blue jacket.

Then Mr. McGregor tried
to trap Peter with a sieve!

Peter wriggled out but he
lost his jacket and shoes.

Peter jumped into a watering-can.

Mr. McGregor was looking for him underneath the flowerpots.

Then Peter jumped out
of a window and knocked
over some flowerpots.
He got away!

Mr. McGregor was tired
of running after Peter.

He went back to his work.

Peter heard the *scritch*,
scratch of Mr. McGregor
gardening. He climbed on to
a wheelbarrow and looked
across the garden.

He could see the gate!

Peter ran as fast as he could go. Mr. McGregor saw him but Peter didn't care. He slipped under the gate and was safe at last.

When Peter got home, he was so tired that he flopped down on to the floor.

Mrs. Rabbit was cooking. "Where have you been, Peter Rabbit?" she said.

Peter Rabbit was not very well. Mrs. Rabbit put him to bed and made him some tea.

But Flopsy, Mopsy and
Cotton-tail had bread
and milk and blackberries
for supper.

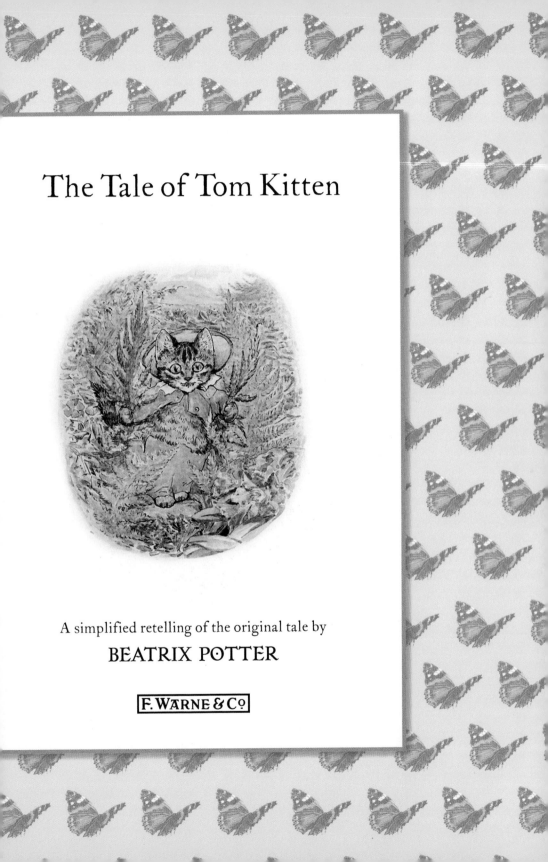

The Tale of Tom Kitten

A simplified retelling of the original tale by

BEATRIX POTTER

F. WARNE & Cº

Here are three little
kittens: Mittens,
Tom Kitten and Moppet.

One day their mother,
Mrs. Tabitha Twitchit, took
them indoors to get ready
for a tea-party.

First she scrubbed their faces. (This kitten is Moppet.)

Then she brushed their fur. (This kitten is Mittens.)

Then she combed their tails
and whiskers. (This kitten is
Tom.)

Mrs. Tabitha Twitchit took
some fine clothes out of the
drawer and dressed her kittens.

The kittens found the clothes
very uncomfortable.
Moppet and Mittens wore
white pinafores.

Tom Kitten's blue suit
was too small for him.
The buttons burst off.

Mrs. Tabitha Twitchit sewed
them on again.

When they were ready,
Mrs. Tabitha Twitchit sent
them outside to play.

"Keep your frocks clean,
children," she said.

In the garden, Tom Kitten
chased a butterfly.

Moppet and Mittens fell
down on the path and made
their clothes dirty.

Then Moppet and Mittens climbed up and sat on the garden wall. "Come along, Tom," they called.

Tom Kitten's buttons had
burst off again.

Moppet and Mittens
helped Tom to climb up the
garden wall.

He lost his hat and his suit was
falling off.

As the kittens sat on the garden wall, three ducks came walking along the road. They were called the Puddle-ducks.

The Puddle-ducks put on Tom's hat.

Moppet, Mittens and Tom
Kitten laughed so much that
they fell off the garden wall.

"Will you help us dress Tom
Kitten?" said Moppet to the
Puddle-ducks.

But one of the Puddle-ducks
put Tom Kitten's clothes
on himself!

"It is a very fine morning,"
said the Puddle-duck.

Then the three Puddle-ducks
walked off along the road
with all of the kittens' clothes.

Their feet went *pit pat,*
paddle pat! Pit pat, waddle pat!

Mrs. Tabitha Twitchit found
her kittens sitting
on the garden wall with
no clothes on.

She was very angry.
She smacked those kittens,
and sent them upstairs!

When Mrs. Tabitha's friends arrived, she told them that her kittens were in bed with the measles.

But the kittens were not in bed at all!

The Puddle-ducks went into a pond and the clothes all came off. They are still looking for them!

The Tale of
Jemima Puddle-Duck

A simplified retelling of the original tale by

BEATRIX POTTER

F. WARNE & CO

This is the story of Jemima Puddle-duck.

Jemima lived on a farm. She wanted to hatch her own eggs but the farmer's wife would not let her.

Jemima's sister, Rebeccah, did not want to hatch her own eggs.

"I would not look after them properly, and neither would you, Jemima," said Rebeccah.

Jemima tried to hide her
eggs so that she could look
after them.

But Jemima's eggs were always
taken away from her.

One day Jemima left the
farm so she could lay her eggs.

She wore a blue bonnet and a
pink shawl.

Jemima Puddle-duck ran
down the hill and then
jumped off into the air.

She flew over the tree-tops
looking for a place to land.

Jemima landed in the wood
and saw someone reading a
newspaper.

"Quack?" said Jemima.

The gentleman looked at Jemima. "Have you lost your way?" he said.

Jemima told the gentleman
that she was trying to find
a place to lay her eggs.

The gentleman said,
"I have a shed. You may lay
your eggs in there."

He opened the door and
let Jemima in.

The shed was full of feathers.
It was very comfortable
and soft. Jemima Puddle-duck
made a nest.

She laid nine eggs.

The next day, the gentleman
said to Jemima, "Let us have
a dinner party."

"Bring some herbs from
the farm and I will make an
omelette."

Jemima met Kep.
He knew those herbs were
for cooking roast duck!

Kep ran to the village and told the puppies.

Jemima went back to
the wood and found
the gentleman.

He spoke in an angry voice. "Check your eggs and then come into my house. Quickly!"

Jemima felt afraid.

Kep and the puppies found the shed in the wood. They shut Jemima in the shed to keep her safe.

Then they chased the
gentleman away.
He never came back.

Kep let Jemima Puddle-duck out of the shed. The puppies rushed in and gobbled up all of the eggs!

Then Kep and the puppies took Jemima back to the farm.

Jemima laid some more eggs
and she was allowed to hatch
them herself. She had four
yellow ducklings.

The Tale of
Benjamin Bunny

a simplified retelling of the original tale by

BEATRIX POTTER

F. WARNE & Co

This is the tale of
Benjamin Bunny.

One morning he sat on a bank
in the woods.

Benjamin Bunny saw a cart
on the road. Mr. and Mrs.
McGregor were in the cart.
They were going out for
the day.

Benjamin ran off to tell his
cousin, Peter Rabbit.

As he peered behind a tree,
Benjamin saw two little ears
sticking out.

It was his cousin, Peter Rabbit,
wrapped in a red handkerchief.

Benjamin sat beside Peter. "Peter, who has got your clothes?"

Peter told him that he had been chased round the garden by Mr. McGregor and had dropped his coat and shoes.

Mr. McGregor was using them for a scarecrow!

"Come along, Peter," said Benjamin. "Mr. and Mrs. McGregor have gone out in their cart. Let us go and find your clothes."

Benjamin and Peter stood
on the garden wall.

They could see Peter's shoes
and coat on the scarecrow.
There was a big green hat on
the scarecrow too.

Benjamin and Peter climbed down a pear tree into the garden. Peter fell down . . . but he was not hurt.

Peter put on his blue coat
and Benjamin put on the
green hat. It was much too
big for him!

Then Benjamin and Peter collected onions for Peter's mother. They put them in the red handkerchief.

As they walked through the garden, Benjamin munched on a lettuce leaf.

But Peter Rabbit felt very scared in Mr. McGregor's garden. He was so scared that he dropped the onions.

As Benjamin and Peter tried
to find their way out of the
garden, they were watched
by some brown mice.

Suddenly, the little rabbits stopped . . .

This is what they saw—
a cat!

They hid underneath a basket. The cat walked over to the basket and . . .

She sat down on top of it!

The cat sat there for
a very long time. Benjamin
and Peter were frightened.

On the wall above the cat, Benjamin's father, old Mr. Bunny, was smoking a pipe. He was looking for his son.

Old Mr. Bunny jumped
down from the wall and
pushed the cat off the
basket.

Then he took the red
handkerchief of onions and
marched those naughty
rabbits home.

That night, the onions were
hung in the kitchen, and
Peter and his sister,
Cotton-tail, folded up the
red handkerchief.

Beatrix Potter was incredibly fond of rhymes.
These poems are from the 1905 and 1917
Appley Dapply collections, rhymes from the
Cecily Parsley collection, and verses from
some of her tales.

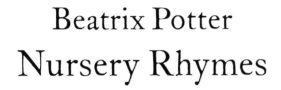

Beatrix Potter
Nursery Rhymes

BEATRIX POTTER

The old woman
who lived in a shoe

You know the old woman
who lived in a shoe?
And had so many children
she didn't know what to do?

I think if she lived
in a little shoe-house –
That little old woman
was surely a mouse!

Diggory Diggory Delvet

Diggory Diggory Delvet!
A little old man in black velvet;
He digs and he delves –
You can see for yourselves
The mounds dug by Diggory Delvet.

Old Mr. Pricklepin

Old Mr. Pricklepin
    has never a cushion to
    stick his pins in,
His nose is black and his
    beard is grey,
And he lives in an ash stump
    over the way.

To Market! To Market!

To Market! To Market!
Now isn't this funny?
You've got a basket,
And I've got some money!
– We went to market
And I spent my money,
Home again! home again!
Little Miss Bunny!

Tabitha Twitchit
is grown so fine

Tabitha Twitchit
is grown so fine
She lies in bed
until half past nine.
She breakfasts on muffins,
and eggs and ham,
And dines on red-herrings
and rasp-berry jam!!

If acorn-cups
were tea-cups

If acorn-cups were tea-cups,
what should we have to drink?
Why! honey-dew for sugar,
in a cuckoo-pint of milk;

With pats of witches' butter
and a tansey cake, I think,
Laid out upon a toad-stool
on a cloth of cob-web silk!

I went into my grandmother's garden

I went into my grandmother's garden,
And there I found a farthing.
I went into my next door neighbour's,
There I bought a pipkin and a popkin,
A slipkin and a slopkin,
A nailboard, a sailboard,
All for a farthing.

Kadiddle,
kadiddle, kadiddle

Kadddle, kadiddle, kadiddle!
Come dance to my dear little fiddle?
(Kadiddle, kadiddle, kadiddle,
Come dancing along down the middle . . .
Oh silly Kadiddle, Kadiddle!).

Hey diddle dinketty

Hey diddle dinketty, poppetty, pet!
The merchants of London they wear scarlet;
Silk in the collar, and gold in the hem,
So merrily march the merchantmen!

Sieve my lady's oatmeal

Sieve my lady's oatmeal,
Grind my lady's flour,
Put it in a chestnut,
Let it stand an hour –
One may rush, two may rush,
Come, my girls, walk under the bush.

Four-and-twenty tailors

Four-and-twenty tailors
Went to catch a snail,
The best man amongst them
Durst not touch her tail;
She put out her horns
Like a little kyloe cow,
Run, tailors, run!
Or she'll have you all e'en now!

Buz, quoth the blue fly

Buz, quoth the blue fly;
hum quoth the bee;
Buz and hum they cry,
and so do we!

In his ear, in his nose,
Thus do you see,
He ate the doormouse,
Else it was thee.

Once I saw a little bird

Once I saw a little bird
Come hop, hop, hop!
So I cried: 'Little bird,
Will you stop, stop, stop?'

And was going to the window
To say, 'How do you do?'
But he shook his little tail
And away he flew.

Three blind mice

Three blind mice, three blind mice,
See how they run!
They all run after the farmer's wife,
And she cut off their tails with a carving knife,
Did you ever see such a thing in your life
As three blind mice!

Pussy-cat sits by the fire

Pussy-cat sits by the fire;
How should she be fair?
In walks the little dog,
Says 'Pussy! are you there?'

'How do you do, Mistress Pussy?
Mistress Pussy, how do you do?'
'I thank you kindly, little dog,
I fare as well as you!'

Goosey, Goosey, Gander,

Goosey, goosey, gander,
Wither will you wander?
Upstairs and downstairs,
And in my lady's chamber!
There I met an old man
That would not say his prayers,
So I took him by the left leg
And threw him downstairs!

Ninny Nanny Netticoat

Ninny Nanny Netticoat,
In a white petticoat,
With a red nose –
The longer she stands,
The shorter she grows.

What could this be?

Answer: A candle

We have a little garden

We have a little garden,
A garden of our own,
And every day we water there
The seeds that we have sown.

We love our little garden,
And tend it with such care,
You will not find a faded leaf
Or blighted blossom there.

This pig went to market

This pig went to market;
This pig stayed at home;
This pig had a bit of meat;
And this pig had none;
This little pig cried
'Wee! Wee! Wee!
I can't find my way home.'

Tom, Tom the piper's son

Tom, Tom the piper's son
Stole a pig and away he ran!
But all the tune that he could play,
Was 'Over the hills and far away!'

Tom with his pipe made such a noise,
He called up all the girls and boys –
And they all ran to hear him play
'Over the hills and far away!'

Ladybird, ladybird,
Fly away home

Ladybird, ladybird,
Fly away home,
Your house is on fire
And your children all gone;
All except one
And her name is Ann,
And she crept under
The pudding pan.

Publisher's Note
Nursery Rhymes taken from Beatrix Potter's works
From the original manuscript of *The Tailor
of Gloucester*:
I went into my grandmother's garden; Hey diddle
dinketty; Sieve my lady's oatmeal; Four-and-twenty
tailors, Buz quoth the blue fly; Once I saw a little bird.
From the 1905 *Appley Dapply* collection:
The old woman who lived in a shoe; Diggory Diggory
Delvet; Old Mr. Pricklepin; To Market! To market!;
Tabitha Twitchit is grown so fine; Kadiddle, kadiddle,
kadiddle; If acorns were teacups.
From *Cecily Parsley's Nursery Rhymes*:
Three blind mice; Goosey, Goosey, Gander; Pussy-cat
sits by the fire; Nanny Nanny Netticoat; We have
a little garden.
From *The Tale of Pigling Bland*:
Tom Tom the piper's son.
From *The Tale of Mrs. Tittlemouse*:
Ladybird, ladybird, fly away home.